EASY READERS MONSTERS 2013

Lagonegro, Melissa author.
Monster games /

08/30/13

Dear Parent:

Congratulations! Your child is taking the first steps on an exciting journey. The destination? Independent reading!

STEP INTO READING® will help your child get there. The program offers five steps to reading success. Each step includes fun stories and colorful art. There are also Step into Reading Sticker Books, Step into Reading Math Readers, Step into Reading Phonics Readers, Step into Reading Write-In Readers, and Step into Reading Phonics Boxed Sets—a complete literacy program with something for every child.

Learning to Read, Step by Step!

Ready to Read   Preschool–Kindergarten
• big type and easy words • rhyme and rhythm • picture clues
For children who know the alphabet and are eager to begin reading.

Reading with Help   Preschool–Grade 1
• basic vocabulary • short sentences • simple stories
For children who recognize familiar words and sound out new words with help.

Reading on Your Own   Grades 1–3
• engaging characters • easy-to-follow plots • popular topics
For children who are ready to read on their own.

Reading Paragraphs   Grades 2–3
• challenging vocabulary • short paragraphs • exciting stories
For newly independent readers who read simple sentences with confidence.

Ready for Chapters   Grades 2–4
• chapters • longer paragraphs • full-color art
For children who want to take the plunge into chapter books but still like colorful pictures.

STEP INTO READING® is designed to give every child a successful reading experience. The grade levels are only guides. Children can progress through the steps at their own speed, developing confidence in their reading, no matter what their grade.

Remember, a lifetime love of reading starts with a single step!

Step into Reading, Random House, and the Random House colophon are registered trademarks of Random House, Inc.

Visit us on the Web!
StepIntoReading.com
randomhouse.com/kids

Educators and librarians, for a variety of teaching tools, visit us at RHTeachersLibrarians.com

ISBN 978-0-7364-3106-4 (trade) — ISBN 978-0-7364-8134-2 (lib. bdg.)

Printed in the United States of America   10 9 8 7 6 5 4 3 2 1

Random House Children's Books supports the First Amendment and celebrates the right to read.

MONSTER GAMES

By Melissa Lagonegro

Illustrated by the Disney Storybook Artists

Random House New York

It is time
for the Scare Games!

Mike and Sulley join
the OK team.

Don is the leader.

He wears glasses.

Squishy is shy.

He has five eyes.

Terri and Terry
are brothers.
They have one body
and two heads.

Art is fuzzy and purple.

Five other teams are
in the Scare Games, too.

The RORs are
a mean team.

The PNKs wear
pink and purple.

The JOX play football.

The EEKs like
to work out.

The HSS team
is tough.

It's time
for the first game!
The teams line up.

Mike and Sulley run
ahead of their team.
The JOX team is out!

Next the teams sneak
past a librarian.
She sees the OKs!

The OKs get their flag.

The EEKs are out!

The OKs practice
as a team.

They work hard.

The third game

is a maze.

The OKs finish!

The PNKs are out.

Next the teams hide.

The OKs work together.

No one finds them!

The HSS team is out.

Only two teams are left.

Which one will win?